KU-246-872

ROSE'S GARDEN

Peter H. Reynolds

WALKER BOOKS
AND SUBSIDIARIES
LONDON · BOSTON · SYDNEY · AUCKLAND

Leabharlann
Chontae Uíbh Fhailí
JBR
11/11532
11/320

Rose was a dreamer.
An adventurer.
She explored the world in her fantastic teapot.

Rose collected seeds from every place
she visited to remember it by.

The teapot became heavy and brimmed with seeds.

"It is time to plant my garden."

There in the distance was a big, bustling city by the sea.

"Welcome, friend. Sail upriver. It's lovely there,"
the harbourmaster called down to Rose.

"Thank you. I think I'll explore the city first," said Rose.

She soon found herself
in the busiest part of the city.

And there she spotted a dusty, forgotten stretch of earth.

Hmmm, Rose pondered. *This little patch needs some colour.*

Rose began to prepare the soil, imagining what
a different, colourful place this could be.

When she went to gather her seeds from the teapot,
she noticed a flock of birds flying away from it.

The birds seemed full and happy.

"Oh, no!"

Rose slipped into the teapot and carefully gathered
the few remaining seeds.

She tucked them inside her pocket, then hurried from the dock.

Rose planted her seeds and waited. Patiently.

But nothing seemed to happen.

The rains of spring made the soil too wet.

The heat of summer made the ground too dry.

The chill of autumn came too early.

She waited through the snowy winter.

The snow melted. The ground warmed.
Still Rose waited – determined that her seeds would wake up.

Word spread of Rose's faith in her garden.

One warm spring day, a girl approached Rose with a present.
It was a paper flower.

"I made it myself, for your garden," the girl said, beaming.
"Thank you!" said Rose.

The next day, a boy appeared with his own handmade flower.

Rose was delighted.
"It will be in good company when my own flowers bloom!"

Day after day, more children came to visit,
each with a paper flower.

They all told stories about coming to this city ... having journeyed
from all over the world, like seeds carried on a breeze.

Before long, the garden was filled with colour … glorious colour.
Thousands of flowers – each one made of paper.
Rose marvelled.

As she waded among them, she heard a sound. A buzzing.
She noticed a bee gently land on one of the flowers.

She peered closer. This flower was not made of paper!
She breathed in its sweet perfume.

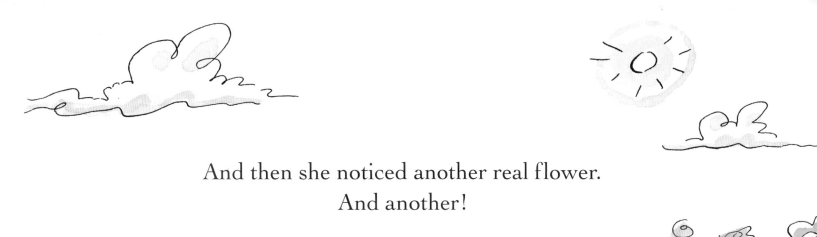

And then she noticed another real flower.
And another!

Each flower, real or paper, had appeared around her because Rose believed. Her faith had gathered a garden – and the stories of a city.

Rose realized then that her travels were over. She was home.

Here in Rose's garden.
Everybody's garden.